ADORING ALEXIS

A SLICE-OF-LIFE SHORT STORY

LOVE WARS SERIES
BOOK 2.5

MICHELLE MARS

Copyright © 2023 by Michelle Mars

No part of this book may be reproduced in any form or by any electronic or mechanical means, including information storage and retrieval systems, without written permission from the author, except for the use of brief quotations in a book review.

This is a work of fiction. Names, characters, places, and incidents, are products of the author's imagination or are used fictitiously. Any resemblance to actual events, locales, organizations, or persons, living or dead, is entirely coincidental.

Cover design by http://bookcovercouture.com

Edited by Jen Graybeal

❀ Created with Vellum

This story goes out to a very good friend, you know who you are, who adores a certain person in the world, you know who they are. Love you, my friend!

This is also an ode to those days when the universe aligns in just the right way so you try on something that suits you perfectly even in fluorescent lighting and it defines a special moment in your life.

Lastly, this book is about friendships. Those that mean everything. Those that bring you comfort. Those that make you laugh. And, occasionally, those that evolve into something more.

PROLOGUE: LOGS

Prologue: Logs

From: Sean.Buttler@gobblemail.com
To: iByte@ibytemore.com
Re: Glad to see you're okay

Hey Jack,

It's been a roller coaster ride watching everything going on between you and your alien. I was happy to read that human relocation is indefinitely on hold. Such a relief. It sounds like an interesting story. Every vampire I know is celebrating, for obvious reasons. What a disaster that would have been.

As you might recall, my two-year vampire rebirth anniversary is tomorrow. Once again, thank you for helping me through your blog and friendship to find my new normal. Finding your iByte site as a newly-made, orphaned vampire was/is a lifesaver. I'm grateful.

In honor of my rebirth, my best friend, Alexis—who thinks she's being slick—is planning a surprise for me. What she doesn't know is that I have plans, too. I'm finally making my move. Wish me luck. I hope I'll continue to hear good things from your blog or the news. If you need anything, don't forget we're all out here and ready to help.

Otherwise, everything is pretty boring around the good old STL. Well, as boring as my life ever gets.

Yours,
Sean

[1]

KINDLING

The day Sean Butler died was a fucked-up day to figure out he was in love with his best friend.

He'd had plenty of experience chasing a rush—fast cars, skydiving, and firefighting—but his rush of feelings was something he hadn't been prepared for.

Alexis Cavill was his ride-or-die. He'd known for years that he loved her. How could he not? They'd been inseparable ever since their last names landed them together in the school line-up. Their pictures graced every yearbook side-by-side, with coordinating outfits, shared poses, or even high-fiving across photos. So... he'd always loved her. But when he realized he was *in* love with her, that rush was more exciting *and* more terrifying.

The day he'd decided to tell Alexis he was *in* love with her things went so very wrong. Thinking back on how excited and nervous he'd been, it was no surprise the damn vamp got the drop on him. One minute he was working out the words he would use and the next he was waking up in her home, the vamp that is. She'd suggested him asleep. It was a rather uncomfortable way to wake up, with a strange woman with her mouth attached to your neck. Quite a way to find out vampires are real but he reacted with the speed and agility firefighters are known for. He wished that were the real story anyway. The truth was that she'd already drained him immobile so he basically woke up long enough to notice his own demise.

That was true until she stuck her bloody wrist in his mouth and shit got weird from there. Long story short, tada, he was a vampire and his maker seemed to think they were going to make a lovely couple. She really should have asked him on a date first because when he told her his heart was spoken for, she raged toward the door to go find Alexis and take her out. There was no way he could let that happen. But, keeping in mind, that he was a brand new vampire and had no idea what his strength would be like when he grabbed her to pull her back, she might have flown backward directly into the giant fireplace she had blazing since it was the dead of winter. As she vampire-version-died, the irony was not lost on him since he was usually saving people from fires. He'd spent a few days telling Alexis that he'd gotten sick and couldn't meet up while he educated himself, from sources like iByte, on what it meant to be, well, vampire-him.

His dilemma was that he couldn't possibly tell Alexis that he loved her on the same day he told her he was a bloodsucker. The timing sucked. *"Hey, I know we've known each other almost our whole lives, but now that I stare longingly at the pulse in your throat, I also love you and want to share my non-life with you."* Yeah. Every woman's dream declaration.

Two years later, he still hadn't figured out exactly what words to use to tell her how he felt. Was he supposed to say it before or after she stole bags of blood… for him… from her job… in a mobile blood donation truck… where she was a phlebotomist? He hated that she did that for him, but since he didn't want to brainwash and bite any undeserving people, he had to supplement in-between hunting for douchebags with the occasional iron-rich to-go bag. It just felt wrong to lay down feelings, while she was forced, out of loyalty, into a life of crime.

On top of that, what if she didn't want to be a vampire? Or what if she wanted kids? They both liked kids, at a distance, that is, but most people eventually do want some. At least, that was what society said. You grew up with some magical clock poised to hit you in the head when it was time to procreate. The fact that he had never been hit by that clock in all his thirty years didn't mean that it wouldn't have ever happened. Right? And while Alexis had never seemed to have been smacked upside her life with that particular clock didn't mean she would want to forgo having it as an option. Right?

After two years of loving her and suppressing his desire to turn her neck into his own personal Slurpee while she rode his cock, he'd decided it was time. Time to confess and hope that it didn't ruin everything between them.

Twenty-two years of friendship on the line, but no pressure. He attempted to look at it as just another one of his risks. One step and he'd be leaping away from the safety of the airplane. Free-falling while hoping his tandem partner didn't disconnect their harnesses leaving him to plummet alone. *Way to psyche yourself out, dumbass.*

He must have grunted at that thought because Jared, another firefighter with his crew, yelled over the siren noise, "Did you say something?"

Well, damn. He knew better than to bring his baggage with him once the alarm went off. Rookie mistake. So he replied, "No. Just cleared my throat. Sorry." It was time to focus. No more distractions. As the fire truck sped through the streets, he set it all aside. He could focus on his future with Alexis... later.

[2]

PIT

Fifteen minutes earlier…

Alexis looked at her reflection in the mirror of the dressing room with the godawful lighting and wondered if her dress said, *"I've wanted you for a long time, and it's killing me to only be your friend,"* or if it said, *"I'm a damn fool for ruining the best friendship I ever had."* Probably a damn fool, but she wasn't backing out now. She'd put off admitting how she felt for too long. Everything had always been so easy between them, but lately—okay, not that lately, more like ever since he told her that he turned into a vampire—things had been shifting.

What had always felt like the most solid and fundamental relationship she'd ever had with her BFF had started to feel uncomfortable. Ill-fitting even. It wasn't because he was a vampire—though, admittedly, that had come as quite a shock. Who could possibly imagine they would end up resembling one of her beloved paranormal romances?

The real problem was that she had to keep her distance or else she would pounce on him. Not like she used to in a friendly way. No. More of the *Take me, bite me, fuck me until my soul exits my body* variety. Definitely *not* what friends do. Definitely. Not. Why was she doing this again?

Her fingertips caressed her neck on the very spot she'd dreamed, many times over, about Sean biting her. She'd speculated about how it might feel. How he might feel. His teeth. His mouth. The pain. The pleasure. Since he'd told her about his heightened vampiric senses, which included smell, she'd kept her distance and her thoughts mostly in check when he was near to avoid the inevitable panty-wetting. Where she used to be able to curl up with him on the couch and heckle bad reality TV often resulting in an impromptu sleepover, she now found herself rigid and keeping her distance.

Tonight, though, panty-wetting was definitely on her to-do list. She bit her lip and attempted to clean up her thoughts as she felt her panties grow damp. Good thing there was no hot vampire best friend around now.

Her reflection didn't help her damp situation any, because—she had to say it—she was a vampire's wet dream. The one-shoulder dress design highlighted exactly where he should direct his mouth. No one ever accused her of being subtle. The dark red was set off stunningly against her dark brown skin. It clung to her breasts and the flair of her hips, curved around her slightly rounded abdomen and showcased her ass like any good mini-dress should. She'd caught Sean staring at some of her assets longer than he used to, with what she hoped was longing or at least desire.

She could work with desire.

Yep. She had found the perfect dress to commemorate the day her best friend became the undead. Finding out had been a conversation and a half. Sean had made a joke out of it because of course he did.

He'd sat her down and then sat next to her holding her hands. "Knock. Knock."

A little exasperated she replied anyway, "Who's there?"

"Vampire."

"Vampire who?"

"Vampires are real and one is sitting right in front of you."

"I don't get it. Are you feeling okay?" He got a look for that one but then went on to explain and she had been torn between anger at the vampire who turned him, shock at well, hello, vampires exist, and grief.

That was the day she had almost lost him. It was the day that opened her eyes... even if she hadn't recognized right away what the new feelings were. Between grief and anger, she found jealousy. That bitch vampire tried to steal her man. Good thing the vamp was dead because if she wasn't, Alexis was going to have to hunt her ass down. It wasn't enough to say anything, though because there was also fear. The fear of losing her best friend by making it weird between them had been too real.

None of that now. She reached around to check the price tag. As she did, she gave herself a pep talk. She was done living for fear. She was going to live for— What the hell? Who pays $1950 for some-thing that has so little material it could pass for a swimsuit? It might be the perfect dress, but Sean was simply going to have to bite her in something less "right." There was no way she was going to be able to afford it on her phlebotomist's salary. She enjoyed her job, but it was not a lucrative calling. That didn't bother her... she was doing just fine, but she wasn't doing *that* fine.

Sad but resigned, and a little panicked at even having something that expensive on her body, Alexis reached behind her to get at the zipper. Unfortunately, the clingy dress was kind of like a clingy rela-tionship... Easy to get into, but so hard to get out of. She stretched her arms over and under behind her back to no avail. The material had somehow gotten tighter. Why would a dress get tighter? She was beginning to feel like someone had vacuum-sealed her into this damn perfect dress. What if she couldn't get this fucking thing off before hurting it and then was forced to buy it?

Nope. "Not today, Satan."

Alexis was going to get out of this dress. Centering herself, she took a calming breath to counter her overly restrained heaving bosoms. She pulled the dress up to her waist so she could brace one leg up on the seat in the dressing room. Like a gymnastic feat from Simone Biles, she threw her arm back *hard,* angling her body in the most uncomfortable ways.

She almost had it when the sound of an alarm blaring

throughout the Lacy's department store made her jump and lose her tenuous grip on the zipper.

No! No! No! She had to get this damn thing off before she left the store.

She reached back again with one arm, bracing the other against the wall, all the while seeking divine intervention, and "Yes!" The zipper began to inch down like the parting of the Red Sea. *Hallelujah! Let my breasts go.*

There was no explaining what happened next, even to herself. Her adrenaline riding high to the sound of the alarm, twisted within an inch of her life, wearing what had begun to feel like a cocoon of death instead of the perfect dress, while balanced on one foot, somehow... she had a sudden, and very powerful sneeze. The propulsion of the sneeze, like one of Wile E. Coyote's rockets, sent her flying back. She reached out to grip onto something but was only able to find a hanger, which snapped as she tumbled.

Pain flared as her head struck the wall behind her. And an even worse pain as she simultaneously felt the sharp edge of the hanger rip into the dress at her thigh. Alexis had two final thoughts before everything went dark. The first... Sean was never going to see her in the now-damaged perfect dress despite her having to pay for it. The second... she never even had a chance to find the right matching shoes. *Dangit!*

When she came awake sometime later, she thought she must be hallucinating. She was staring up into the blue-gray eyes she had been dreaming about for the last couple of years. Eyes as familiar to her as her own. "Sean? Are you okay? You look terrible."

[3]

WOOD

If Sean could bite the idiot who decided it would be funny to pull the fire alarm, he would. Okay. Maybe he wouldn't, but he sure wanted to. When they arrived at the shopping center—the location of their call—it turned out to be a false alarm. As they were in the process of resetting the alarm, cussing out their frustrations, a sales clerk tentatively began to speak to him.

"Excuse me, sir. I need your help." He turned fully toward her as she continued, "There was a woman who had gone into the dressing room before the alarm went off. I went in to make sure she made it out and found her crumpled on the ground."

Sean was about to request Sloane, one of the women on his crew, join him to help with the unconscious woman in the dressing room. He stopped when he caught the tiniest trace of a scent he knew all too well.

"Take me to her, please." Sean couldn't know for sure, but of course he did. The scent. He indicated to his chief that he was checking something out and got a nod of approval.

What was Alexis doing here? And… why was she unconscious? She better fucking be okay. She had to be. Tonight was their night.

He asked the clerk as they walked to the dressing room about the health of the woman. They arrived at the stall and there she was. His Alexis. He knelt beside her, going through the motions of checking for a pulse since he already heard she had one. Still, he could scent her blood in the air, causing his teeth to elongate and his body energy to rise against his will. He spoke to the clerk without looking her way. "Could you please bring me a glass or bottle of water?"

"Of course. I'll be right back," he heard as she scurried away.

He gently felt the back of Alexis' head, through her abundant, brown curls, and found the spot where she must have hit it. She moaned and shifted. Yeah. He bet that hurt. Her eyes fluttered open and, in gloriously Alexis fashion, she asked if *he* was okay. Him. "It's you I'm worried about."

He inspected the rest of her to ensure nothing was broken and that was when he realized what she was wearing. More to the point, that there wasn't much of it to begin with, and the not-much-of-it that there was had bunched up at her waist.

Her blue cotton underwear was the only thing on the lower half of her. The same underwear where he could scent her arousal now that he wasn't so focused on the smell of her blood. His gaze slid down over the smooth skin on her thick thighs, and he gulped. Nothing had ever looked so appetizing.

He'd planned to declare his feelings and seduce her later that night. That ship had sailed when a low, guttural growl escaped his lips as he returned to staring at the juncture of her thighs. His unruly teeth extended completely and his baser instincts took over. "That's my pussy." As soon as the words were out, he wished he could use his power to turn back time. *I can't believe I said that.*

"Excuse me?" Alexis's chagrin was evident in the tension he could feel radiating from her whole body.

"I can't believe I said that." He couldn't blame her incredulous tone. What did he expect would happen?

"Did you seriously claim my pussy without even a please and thank you, while I lie here injured?" She gave him the, "What are you? A dumb-ass?" look and continued, "I know my mama taught you better than that. She's probably rolling in her grave. Put those teeth away and help me up." She gripped one of his hands and braced as though he was about to yank her up.

Shit. He'd single-handedly torpedoed all of his plans for the night. Even his predator-side felt the sting of Alexis's response to his ill-timed words. His teeth receded back in shame. As she struggled to get up, he said, "I don't think you should move until I can fully inspect you."

"I think you've inspected me enough, don't you?" Her words dripped with innuendo this time.

He couldn't think clearly. She'd left him torn between desire and concern. "I—"

"Sean. If you don't help me up, I'm going to be forced to do it on my own."

And she would, too. "Not until you've had some of my blood."

"Ew!" Her lip curled up in disgust.

"Listen, we both know you might have a concussion. We won't have to worry about that if you take some of my blood. It's your choice. Drink up or I walk you over to the paramedics." There was no way she wanted to spend the next hours being checked over and coddled and watched. He could practically see the shudder she had when she thought of it.

"Okay, fine. But also, ew."

He sliced his wrist and fed her some of his blood. For such a minor thing, it wouldn't take much to heal her. He took comfort that there was a marked difference in her complexion and vitality right away. "Better?"

"Yes. I'd had a mild headache before which is gone. My taste-buds, my wallet, and my hurt pride are the only things still damaged."

He stood and carefully helped her up, watching for any signs she hadn't drunk enough, but she seemed genuinely okay.

Shock gripped him as she cut off his words by putting her mouth on his. *Wait. Wait. Hold up.* Alexis had her mouth on his. Apparently, his brain was the foggy one. She seemed perfect.

Or… maybe she felt perfect? All he knew was that she was

kissing him. Her arms wound firmly around his neck. And… what was he waiting for?

He pulled her in close and sucked at her lip, sliding his tongue out and asking permission to enter her mouth. She didn't only grant it to him. Nope. Her tongue came ready to tussle.

Fuck yeah!

He was so hungry for her—starved—and she tasted so damn good. A mix of what he'd imagined she'd taste like based on her scent, but, also, so much more. As they kissed, it was like swirling an expensive whiskey to make sure it hit every note on your pallet. And, like a strong whiskey, the taste and feel of her intoxicated him.

He couldn't remember lifting her by her bare-except-underwear ass nor when her long legs wrapped themselves around his hips. All he knew was that the core of her was cradling the only piece of him doing any thinking. And boy, it had a lot of thoughts like, *Take her*, or *Damn she's hot*, or *Fuck, yeah*, or—

A throat clearing from only a few feet away jolted him back into full awareness. He nearly dropped Alexis in his rush to right them. He didn't, of course. Drop her that is. No way would he risk injuring her even more. The clerk, on the other hand, was lucky. His power, already high from lust, had almost exploded out of him at being startled. Wouldn't that have been a bad scene?

Wanting to cover up their indiscretion, he issued his power out gently, stared into the disapproving clerk's eyes, and said, "You've only now returned. All you'll remember is that you brought the water, and you found us standing in the changing room waiting for you."

The clerk blinked in confusion for a moment. Sean took that moment to make sure Alexis righted herself, including, disappointingly, having to pull down the skirt of her dress. Her very tight, wickedly sexy dress. He diverted himself from those thoughts by turning back to the clerk. She smiled at him and offered him the glass of water.

"Thank you."

He took the proffered water and handed it to Alexis. She stared at it as though she didn't recognize water at first. But then, she brought it up to her lips and her eyes met his over the rim. And damn, her look made some pretty seriously dirty promises. He'd never seen that look in Alexis' beautiful brown eyes before, and seeing it now sucked since he couldn't act on it. He had a job to do, an onlooker to appease, a boss to report to.

He threw back a look that hopefully said, *Behave*.

She didn't.

[4]

MATCH

Walking around with wet panties was not okay. Not when she had to assure everyone that she was well, sign away medical help, and practically cry through paying for the dress she still wore. She'd enjoyed secretly flirting with Sean—as he glared—knowing he could still smell her across the room, putting him on edge. Well, good. He should be on edge. After kissing her and holding her like that... how dare he?

She wasn't mad about the kiss. She was mad that he kissed her like *that* and hadn't done it sooner. How dare he keep all that under wraps? Not tonight, though. Tonight would be a new start for them.

Sean left with his crew, heading back to the station, but she knew he'd make a quick turnaround to meet her.

She raced to his apartment, abandoning all her other plans for the night. Using the key he'd given her ages ago, Alexis entered. One hand closed the door behind her as she looked at her purse to make sure she put the keys inside the right pocket.

"Oomph!"

A solid wall blocked her. She looked up and it was Sean. "What? How? How are you here?"

He pointed at himself and smirked. "Vampire."

She deflated a bit. Damn. "Why are all my plans failing today?"

He must have heard the frustration in her voice because she found herself in his arms. Not in the way she'd originally planned but in a comforting, all-engulfing hug instead. His black hair curled around his ear, tickling her cheek, and he smelled like home.

He whispered, "What's wrong, and how can I make it better?"

She took a deep breath and said the scariest thing she'd ever said. "I'm in love with you. I had grand plans to tell you tonight, but now my plans are all fucked. I didn't even get to put on my sexy underwear instead of my cotton-forgotten." She rested her forehead on his shoulder and her hands on his hips. Taking a deep breath, she released it in acceptance.

His chest moved, lifting her head. His arms loosened. Was he pulling back? Was he about to tell her their earlier kiss was a mistake? She hoped not. She was missing the comfort of his embrace already. She didn't have to miss it for long, though, because he moved his hands up to cup her face. His deep blue-gray eyes bored into hers with so much intensity she was compelled toward humor. "Hey. Buddy. My breasts are down here." She indicated her chest, barely contained in the soul-stealing, perfect dress.

His seriousness dissolved with a snort and an ogle. *That's better.*

"Yes, they are. In fact, I don't think I've ever tried talking to your breasts before. Excuse me."

The bastard actually began to kneel, as though he was going to start a conversation with her boobs, and she was going to lose her damn mind waiting for him to respond to her proclamation. He didn't stop for a chat, though. She let out an involuntary scream as he scooped her up into his arms and carried her off to bed.

"I'm sorry that all of your plans were ruined. If it makes you feel any better, I had plans of my own for tonight. I've abandoned almost all of them. The only plans that matter, though, overlap with yours. I'm in love with you, Alexis Cavill, and I look forward to telling your breasts all about it… personally."

Her heart picked up its rhythm as he placed her on her feet and began to reach for her dress. *Hell no!* "Uh-uh. You will not be manhandling this dress. No, sir. Did you see how much I paid for it?

And it already has a small rip I have to fix. Just unzip the back for me please."

His deep chuckle warmed her as she turned. He slid the zipper down, grazing his mouth across her shoulder. Oh. That felt *good*. A sensual shiver ran the length of her spine, and she gasped. Sean trailed his nose and lips along her skin until he reached her neck. He nipped lightly and she could feel his sharp, elongated teeth. *Oh, yeah.*

This was why she wanted the dress in the first place.

"Bite me."

"Um…Are you sure?"

"Yes."

"What about your dress?"

Yeah. Okay. True. She swiftly but carefully pulled her hand out of the sleeve, letting the bodice drop around her hips. Grabbing her underwear along with the dress, she pushed them down, bending her over, ass in the air. This elicited a grunt from Sean.

As she straightened back up, Sean whispered under his breath, "So fucking perfect," and knelt behind her, holding her hips in place with firm hands. His mouth trailed kisses up one of her thighs, paused over one butt cheek, and bit. Not to break skin but so he could suck. "Sean! Are you marking my ass?"

He stopped, and with arousing satisfaction, said, "Most definitely. I love your ass. Now stop talking and let me worship you already."

"Could you worship me a little faster?"

"Whatever the lady wants."

[5]

FLAME

Sean couldn't believe he was finally feeling and tasting the woman he had been longing for, who had stolen his heart, who he loved beyond words. And yet, getting to say the words, to say how they felt about each other was such a relief.

Relief was not what drove him now though. That was hunger. A hunger to know Alexis as intimately physically as he did spiritually. To that end, he continued his way up her back with kisses, licks, and nips until he was poised over her neck again. He hesitated briefly, but she demanded again, "Bite me."

He wound his arms around her, resting one palm lightly over her pussy while the other took a firm grip of her breast. The moment he bit into her flesh, he redirected Alexis' thoughts from the pain by pinching her nipple and playing his fingers through her folds. Her body relaxed into his embrace as he released the optional pleasure chemical in his bite.

He continued to knead one breast and then the other, pinching and tugging at her firm nipples. Gazing over her shoulder and down her body, his mouth watered with the intense desire to suck and bite at her beautiful brown areolas. With his other hand, he delved into her entrance, gathering some of the wetness he found there and using it to lubricate his finger as it circled her clit. Her body responded instantly to his touch. He tried a few different patterns, speeds, and levels of firmness until he landed on the one that made her wetness multiply, a gasp escaping from her lips.

"Sean. Sean. I want your cock." Her voice was husky with need.

He licked the bite closed and whispered in her ear, "You'll get my cock. Don't worry. I've been wanting to fuck you for two long years. My cock will come out to play soon. But first, I want to watch you come in my arms. I want to see the pleasure on your face as you come apart for me. Only then will I be pulling out my cock. So… How badly do you want it?"

The whole time he spoke, he continued to play her body to his tune. He could tell by her rapid breathing and the rush of her blood under his touch that she was close.

He growled, "If you want me inside you sooner, I suggest you come for me."

"I would, if you moved your hand a little bit faster. I need more." Her body quivered. "Do something. Please!"

So he did.

He pinched her clit as he said, "I love you."

Her guttural response to his declaration and her subsequent, "Oh fuck!" as she came was the sexiest thing he'd ever heard. He held her tight as she went limp.

Sean wasn't able to wait another second. He needed her so much. He carefully flung her onto the bed, then worried about her head. "Oh shit! Are you okay?"

Alexis laughed. "I told you. I'm fine and happy that you're so eager."

He ripped off his clothes at a speed no human could track. She gasped in surprise as he climbed on top of her and positioned his cock at her entrance. She wrapped her legs around his waist, opening to him completely. "God I want to fuck you so bad. Tell me again."

She knew what he wanted to hear, and she gave it to him. "I love you." Then she continued with, "I also love your cock. So… Get in here."

He chuckled. "What do you know of my cock?"

"Is it a part of you?"

"Clearly"

"Then I love it. Now stop talking and introduce us."

He was glad to see they wouldn't lose the essence of who they were. He kissed her deeply as he thrust home. She was so ready for him. So wet. So hot. So his. His best friend. And now his lover. His.

"Oh God, Sean. I want to be with you for eternity. You feel so good. So right."

That stopped him in his tracks, mid-thrust. He leaned back to look her in the eyes. "What? That's a big step."

"I know. And… I'm sure."

He was sure too. Being with Alexis was the only eternity he could picture for himself. That was all the more reason to do it right. "We have plenty of time to figure it out. I want to confirm that we do it safely, perhaps with advice from Jack. I want it to be perfect. Special for you."

"I'm fine waiting. I'm not in a hurry, but I thought you should know my intentions."

"And here I thought you only wanted me for my cock and my bite."

"Those too, and don't you think at least one of those should be busy right now?"

He didn't answer in words. Instead, he rocked into her, finding a rhythm that worked for them both. With each thrust, his power climbed. He'd learned about the vampiric power escalation that happened during sex from all the literature Jack had provided, but this was the first time he was able to experience it himself.

Alexis stuck her fingers in his mouth, coating them in his saliva, and reached down between their bodies, using them to play vigorously with her clit. Sexy as fuck. He was freed up to take full enjoyment of her breasts, licking between them, enjoying every moan he elicited from her lips. Sensing when she was on the precipice, he engulfed one of her nipples in his mouth and bit her there as she orgasmed, which caused her to come a second time followed quickly by a third.

With the taste of her, the scent of her, and the feel of her drowning him in sensation, he pumped his hips a few more times and came with a grunt. His first orgasm as a vampire was overwhelming in its intensity and sharing it with Alexis that much more so. In the literal sense, and despite the practical learning he'd done, he was ill-prepared for the experience of shedding the sexual layers of power during orgasm. He grunted again as things shook in the room.

When she caught her breath, she said, "You grunt when you orgasm?"

"What?"

"You heard me."

"And?" This was not the pillow talk he expected.

"And nothing. Grunting is sexy as hell. That's all."

"Noted." He smirked and flipped onto his back, cuddling her to him. "Alexis?"

"Yes?"

"Thank you. I never needed any fancy plans or dresses, though that dress was killer on you. All I really needed was... sex." He looked down and caught her narrow-eyed look and laughed. "The sex *was* really fucking good."

She replied saucily, "You're not wrong."

He gave her a lopsided smile. "Yeah. You know what I needed was you."

She combed her fingers through his hair, which felt incredible. "It feels like it's always been you. I was simply unaware of it before. I never wanted to lose your friendship."

"Exactly. But when I almost died—"

"Yes. When you almost died, everything came into focus—"

"And I would've regretted not loving you in every way that I possibly could."

They were comfortably silent. Absorbing it all.

Sean rolled Alexis onto her back. "Speaking of every way that I can possibly love you." He moved down her body and under the covers, exploring one more way.

He couldn't believe how smoothly things fell together. Planning the perfect time for her transition to a vampire… well… they had plenty of time for that. He would make sure it was as magical as she was. For now, all he wanted was to enjoy every minute they had together in their new couple-dom.

[6]

CATCHING

Alexis woke up wrapped in her best friend's arms and nothing had ever felt so good. It was a good thing that she'd always kept an overnight kit for those days she passed out at his place because passed out about described the state she'd been in after all those orgasms. With superhero swiftness, she'd gotten ready for bed and was out as soon as his warmth enfolded her.

With the sun streaming in, she lifted her head to see if he was still sleeping or awake. She needed visual confirmation since breathing was optional for him and would not be a good indicator. Blue-gray eyes stared back at her and his lips formed the sexiest lopsided smile. She loved that smile so much. It sent her literal heart racing and her metaphorical heart filled with comfy, warm, gooey feelings.

"Good morning," she rasped followed by a yawn and stretch.

"Good morning, snuggle-muffin."

Mid-stretch, Alexis couldn't have held her side-eye back if she'd tried. "Snuggle-muffin? I don't think so."

"Schnuckums?" His eyebrow raised in inquiry.

"Are you serious right now?"

"Bunny?"

"Stop playing with me." She swatted his chest.

Sean grabbed her hand and moved it down his pecs, his abs, and further until he had her hand cupping his cock. "Perhaps you should play with me instead."

"Now *that* I can get behind." She moved her hand along his hard length in slow, deliberate strokes. "But… should I play gently with my new toy?" She moved to hover over him, her mouth above his dick, and spit where her hand was stroking. "Or maybe, I should be a bit rougher?" She began to move faster and with a firmer grip. "Any thoughts?"

"Oh. I definitely have thoug—" He stopped mid-sentence as she took the tip of him into her mouth while continuing to move her hand.

After swirling her tongue along the top, licking up the treat she found there, she lifted off and said, "You were saying?"

He groaned. "Was I?"

"Yes, cupcake, you were." He snorted at her nickname. "But, that's okay. I got you." Since she had a bad gag reflex, she took him a little ways into her mouth and used her hand to play. She couldn't wait to hear the grunt he would make when she succeeded.

Sean carefully pulled her sleep bonnet off and wrapped his hand in her hair, pulling her head back so her mouth popped off his dick. "You want me to come in your mouth? Because if you don't stop, that's what will happen, angel-tits."

It was her turn to snort. "That was kind of the point. If you need to hold on for the ride, that's fine by me. Keep arms and legs inside at all times and get ready to have your cock, I mean mind, blown."

He left his hand in her hair, but when she took him down her throat this time, his head slammed into the pillow and his hips bucked making her gag a bit. She came up for air briefly and then went back to work. It didn't take long before she got exactly what she wanted. With a deep, guttural grunt, Sean came down her throat. She swallowed swiftly trying to take him all down but some escaped from the corner of her mouth. He swiped his thumb across her chin and plopped that escaping bit onto her tongue. That was so damn dirty. So damn sexy.

With his vampire strength and speed, Alexis hadn't even had a chance to register what was happening when she found herself facing the headboard with her hips hovering above his mouth.

He growled at her, "Get your hands on that headboard and do not let go. It's your turn to take a ride. Get your fine ass pussy on my face and don't let up until I make you come. Remember, I don't need to breathe. But, I do need your taste on my tongue right the fuck now." He paused and then added, "Apple-honey-bottom."

She grabbed the top of the headboard and slowly dropped down onto his face as she said, "At least this way, I can shut you up."

She felt his muffled laugh across her pussy lips before his tongue began exploring her folds.

Alexis learned something new that day about her bestie. He had a very agile tongue and he knew how to use it. He tickled at her clit with the tip. Used the flat of it to give her long licks. Nipped with his sharp teeth at the hood. But, all of that paled at the discovery of the very length of his tongue as he entered her. *Holy shit!* The sensations were overwhelming. And yet, nothing prepared her for the orgasm that struck her when his teeth pierced the sensitive skin around her clit and released his pleasure chemical.

Two back-to-back orgasms left her utterly and completely spent. She wasn't sure how she found herself snuggled at his side again, but she luxuriated in the moment like a cat in a sunbeam. Thank goodness neither of them were working until tomorrow. "Since neither of us has anywhere to go, what shall we do with the rest of our day?"

"I have some ideas, Alexinator."

That earned him a pillow to the abdomen. Still, she couldn't help but play along, "I'll be back." She jumped up and ran to the bathroom and realized that with a vampire, you never have to worry about morning breath since they don't actually have to breathe if it gets too bad. *Coolio.*

When she came back out, she found Sean in the kitchen wearing nothing but boxers, and the best smell in the world, after Sean of course, already emanating from the oven. Fresh biscuits. Yum. Sean always had some in the freezer ready to bake for the days they ate breakfast for dinner or she stayed the night. They hadn't done that since… She paused and realized she'd avoided staying the night for the last two years and they'd only pulled them out for the nighttime meals. It felt like reclaiming a part of their friendship they'd lost amongst their concern over feeling more for each other.

"What can I help with?"

"Nothing. I got it. Sit and let me take care of you."

He did appear to have it all in-hand. With the biscuits already baking, Sean was busy working on the sausage gravy in one pan and had eggs already cracked and scrambled with cheese in a bowl ready to fry up. "How about I'll be in charge of the coffee? And cake?"

"Cake? Since when do we have cake with breakfast?"

Alexis walked up behind him and grabbed handfuls of his firm butt and squeezed. "Cake is definitely on the menu now."

"Troublemaker."

"Now there is a nickname I could get behind after I enjoy this behind some more." She gave him another squeeze.

"What happened to coffee?" He growled.

"I think we could find more enjoyable ways to stay awake today."

"Does that mean you don't want your breakfast?" He looked over his shoulder at her with an arched brow.

It took only a moment of consideration before she stepped away. "Nah. There's no way I'm passing up my favorite, but after, you should be prepared to get into trouble with me."

"It's a deal."

Hours later, full and fucked, Alexis drifted off to nap, a smile engraved on her face and in her soul.

[7]

INCENDIARY

The next few weeks flew by in a blur for Sean. There were a bunch of seemingly connected fires being set by someone in the vicinity of his firehouse as well as the surrounding areas. Almost every shift was filled with a call-out. As full of fire as his work was getting, his days off were equally so.

He and Alexis couldn't get enough of each other. It was like discovering a new side of himself. Thinking, "I know this person as much as I know myself," but also realizing there are still new depths to plunge. New heights to climb. New curves of her body to explore.

His shifts were hell but his times off were heaven.

During one such break, he walked around his apartment searching for his lover. Peering out at the park behind his place, Alexis was bent over the railing of his deck holding a cup of coffee, enjoying the cool morning. She had been sleeping over every night he was home. Watching her as she closed her eyes to soak in the crisp morning air. She was still wearing her sleep bonnet of purple silk and her classic Superman tank and shorts combo. No woman had ever looked more beautiful.

He walked up behind her, leaning over to cage her in his arms. Aligning their bodies and kissing her neck. Her skin was a combination smell of her delicious cocoa butter and her own essence and underneath that—he could smell her blood, enticing him to bite. To nip. To sip his own morning elixir.

"Good morning, gorgeous. How are you today?" He grazed his teeth gently along the line of her throat, her responding shiver sending his power and desire up a notch.

"Mmmm. Good morning. That feels good." She leaned back into his crotch and wiggled.

He grunted as his partial morning erection grew in intensity and firmness. "Troublemaker."

"You started it. You know what your teeth do to me."

"Do I? What do my teeth do to you?"

With another wiggle of her glorious ass, she hummed. "I'm addicted. The sharp penetration makes me think of every other penetration we enjoy with each other. They're so hard and unyielding. When you tease me with them, it's like you're running your cock along my folds and all I can think about is wanting you to do it. To take me." She leaned her head back exposing her neck to his consideration even more. "To penetrate me and make me a part of you."

He clutched her tighter and growled, "Damn, Purple-Pancake, I could get off to your words alone."

"Don't go ruining the morning with that nickname game of yours," she laughed. "Aren't you thirsty? I know I am."

"You bet I am, but not here."

"There's no one around. No one will see."

He looked around and sure enough, this morning, nothing stirred near their corner unit on the upper floor. Sean supposed most people were probably already at work or school. "You win." After a lick up her neck, from shoulder-neck-junction to ear, and back he gently sunk his teeth into her tender flesh. She gasped softly at first penetration, but with his pleasure chemical released, she moaned right after, grinding even harder back into his now fully erect cock.

"Oh shit!" Alexis jerked away scrambling, leaving the punctures bleeding down her back.

Startled he hissed, "What? What happened? Are you okay?"

He heard from below a solid thud.

"I'm so glad no one was walking around down there. What you were doing felt so good, I lost my grip on my ceramic coffee mug!"

Looking over the edge, seeing it had landed in a patch of thick grass and was still whole, he hugged her tight from behind and licked the bite closed. "Are you grumpier that it fell or that you didn't get to drink it?"

"To drink it of course…"

He chuckled and squeezed her again. "You watered the grass. Does grass like hot coffee you think?" For that he got an elbow in the ribs. "Okay. I know you need it. I'll go make you another cup."

"Thank you." She turned and kissed him getting a tiny bit of blood that must have stayed on his lips from the sudden detachment. It made her look so tasty, it hurt to walk away. He rubbed his thumb across her bottom lip first, though, to collect the small red smear and then put it in his mouth like a kid licking syrup off sticky fingers.

"Yummy. Unlike some people, I don't waste my breakfast drink."

That earned him a playful glare and, as he turned to go make her coffee, an ass slap so he called over his shoulder, "Save that for later."

"Oh. Don't think I haven't thought of some truly dirty things I might want to do with that perfectly sculpted ass."

He looked over his shoulder and sure enough, he found her leering at his backside. "I am not just a piece of meat, you know."

She shook her head but was still watching his butt and also licking her lips. "Maybe not, but I still want to take a bite of it. Mmm. Why haven't I done that yet?" She nodded to herself. "Definitely adding that to the list."

Heading into the kitchen to make another mug of coffee while she continued into the living room, he yelled, "I didn't know there was a list. Maybe we should compare our lists and see what we can check off." The sexy domesticity was one of his favorite changes from their friendship to more.

When he brought her coffee, she took a sip before putting the mug down on the coffee table. "I thought you were desperate to drink that."

In response, she dragged his boxers to his knees, pushed him to sit on the couch, and straddled him. His erection had calmed some when he'd gone to make his lover's extra cup of coffee but turned rock hard again as she climbed on, straddling his hips. He grabbed a handful of her ass, her short-short pajamas riding up and revealing her two luscious globes underneath.

Holding onto his shoulder with one hand, she reached down between them and pushed the thin material of her shorts and briefs to the side. Sliding her warm, wet heat down his length until she had taken all of him inside, maintaining eye contact the whole way.

Not one word was spoken as she began to roll her hips and he was forced to match her rhythm. He'd found Nirvana. When her speed increased, so did his and he gripped her hips to hold on to the most important person in his life. The one who could make eternity sound really fucking good.

[8]

BLAZE

Alexis wasn't sure what had made her throw Sean down on the couch and have her way with him, because it could have been one of a plethora of things. It could be the fact that he looked so sexy in the mornings with his dark hair sticking up at all angles. Probably the fact that he had a body sculpted of hard work, played a part. At the end of the day, while his dick was also mouth-watering, the main reason every time, was the way he loved her. This man had been her always even before he became her everything. And *that* had her hungry for him constantly.

The bruising feeling of his grip on her hips felt so damn good. Like he never wanted to let go. Like he was laying claim to her desire. She rode him, hips jerking, rolling, and bouncing. Each alternative rhythm created a new friction that was sending her toward blissful release. "Sean. Sean. You fill me up so well. I love how you feel inside me."

She leaned her head back and remembered, by the feel of the silk, about her bonnet. She pulled the string at the top unravelling the bow and threw it to the other side of the couch. Her curls were free and Sean took advantage to grasp the hair at the nape of her neck drawing her face to his. He growled into her face, "You take my cock so well. I want nothing more than to fill you up."

With that declaration, he filled her mouth with his tongue as he possessively laid claim to her there as well. His other hand grabbed a handful of her breast as it bounced squeezing the nipple between thumb and forefinger before rolling it. After minutes, hours lost in his kiss, his hand snaked around to the front of her neck and held her still, hovering just above his face like they were sharing breaths. "Now be good, troublemaker, and come for me. I want to feel your pleasure all over my cock." His fingers tightened ever so slightly cutting off her circulation for a moment.

He didn't have to ask her twice. She reached between them and began to play with her clit. She was already strung so tight, a few flicks and she was flying. Right at the height of her orgasm, he moved his thumb and bit her again, and the orgasm refused to end. "Yes! Ah. Yes! Sean!" It was so much better than she ever dreamed.

Sean was roughly pumping up into her and the air around them was electrified with his power. Like touching one of those Van De Graaff electricity generators.

"Alexis!" he said so reverently. And, as expected, she got his sexy grunt right when he finished and everything shook. She collapsed onto his chest, her cheek along his scruffy one.

He nipped her earlobe playfully. "You ma'am are too beautiful for words."

"And you sir quite literally take my breath away. Speaking of breath, when are we turning me into a vampire? Hmm?" She smirked.

"So impatient." He tsked, jokingly. "I'm planning the most memorable vampire-turning day anyone has ever had. You'll make a stunning vampire, you know?"

"I know." Winking at him, she moved her hips ever so slightly and they both groaned.

Sean caged her against his chest and she couldn't imagine anywhere else she wanted to be… mostly. But the fact that she *still* hadn't had her coffee hit hard , so she wiggled her way off of his lap. The disconnect of their bodies was always so sad, but… coffee.

She ran over to the bathroom cleaned up and brought a warm, wet washcloth back to wipe Sean. That accomplished she grabbed up her mug and plopped down to enjoy God's gift to mornings.

"I'll try not to be offended that cuddle time was usurped by coffee." Sean grumped.

"That would be wise for our lasting peace." She winked.

"Order of needs: sex, coffe—"

His cell rang interrupting his list. She sipped and watched him grab his phone with a look of confusion. He answered, putting it up to his ear. "This is Sean." His face changed into concern within moments and he said, "I'll be right there."

When he hung up, she asked, "What's wrong?"

"Another fire," he said as he ran into his bedroom, threw some clothes on, and was heading toward the door. "That makes eight of these types of fires, so they are putting more people on the investigation and calling in backup to make sure every shift is covered. You can stay as long as you want. I'll be in touch when I'm free again."

She grabbed his arm before he stepped out, turning him to her, and framed his face, "You be careful and come back to me."

"Of course." He wrapped his arm around her waist kissing her hard and fast and then he was gone.

Alexis spent the rest of the morning, after drinking her coffee, tidying, and decided to head home. Some inconsequential decisions can alter your whole life. She really should have just stayed in bed.

[9]

INFERNO

Sean was at the end of his freaking rope dealing with this arsonist. They were getting bolder and the instances were getting closer together. And this time… this time they'd struck a warehouse that had some people in it at the time. No one died, but they had to rescue a few of them. It was a good thing he'd been called in, because he wasn't sure how they would have gotten out if he hadn't been able to use his vampiric speed without breathing, when no one was looking, to find some of the victims.

As much as he couldn't wait to get back to Alexis, whom he hoped to find curled up on his couch or in his bed, he wasn't ready to be done for the day. He had picked up the perpetrator's scent at the last location, recognizing the same scent had been in the air at all the other locations as well. It was time for him to go hunting. His heart was in firefighting, but he was also still a vampire, and he was going to behave as one to stop this person before someone actually got hurt.

As he headed out, tracking the criminal, Sean tried to call Alexis, but he couldn't get through to her cell. She probably fell asleep watching the TV too loud again. He sent her one more text alerting her to his late return, turned the sound off, and continued on his mission.

The scent led him to a populated area, which had him on edge. His anxiety multiplied in spiraling succession as he picked up a few other smells in the air. Smoke. *Shit!* But there was another scent that nearly had him in a panic, Alexis. *What the hell is she doing here?* He followed all three to the same spot, a clinic that Alexis volunteered at on some of her days off. "No!"

In the distance, far enough away that only his vampiric hearing could pick up, he made out sirens indicating the fire had already been reported, but there was no way he could wait to go in until they arrived. He closed his eyes and listened for heartbeats, breathing, or any indication of who, where, and how many. What he picked up on that made things go from dire to worse…the six faint heartbeats of people inside who weren't trying to get out.

Before he could move, the scent of gasoline, smoke, and multiple people's blood hit him, and it was moving his way fast. Well, fast for a human. Sean raced to intercept him, noting the gleeful expression on his face before yanking him around and gripping his face so he couldn't look away. Power lashed out causing the man's knees to buckle. "You will forget me completely, you will sit here on the sidewalk, when the police and firemen show up, you will turn yourself in, and you will admit to all of your crimes, all of them. Am I clear?"

The criminal's eyes, glassy from Sean's influence, blinked once and he nodded. "Yes."

That was all of the time he could spare for the low-life. He let go and the man dropped to the sidewalk waiting to carry out Sean's commands.

Within seconds, he zoomed inside the building intent on saving everyone including the love of his life. The fire seemed to be localized toward the back and left side of the building. He moved as fast as he could targeting the sections that had the most fire first, even though Alexis wasn't in that section, and depositing everyone he encountered outside the propped open entry doors. All of the people he rescued were unconscious and bleeding from hits to their heads. Somehow the monster outside had managed to knock them all out.

He deposited the fifth person at the door and could hear the fire crew coming to a stop outside the building. He needed to find Alexis and get them both out of there. Hopefully, she would be in the same shape as all the other victims but with less smoke inhalation. It was why he had saved her for last. The other victims had been where the fire had started. Unfortunately, he had calculated wrong.

Tucked to the back right side of the building, in the kitchen with the door to the backyard, he found her. Not much smoke, he was correct about that. But, now that he was close enough his senses weren't dulled by the thick pollution, all he could smell was blood. It felt like just yesterday he'd found her unconscious in a dressing room, worried at the small scent of her blood. Now, he was downright terrified. The last time paled in comparison to what he found now by infinite magnitudes.

It was clear his baby had put up a fight. Her white lab coat a sea of red from her chest down. Protruding from there, a wicked-looking butcher knife. "No! Alexis!" He yelled for her as he dropped down next to her limp body. He listened intently for a heartbeat, and faint as it was, it was still there. No human technology could save her now. He'd been doing his job long enough to know that.

Think!

He needed to remember what Jack had taught him about making a vampire and healing. Earth and blood.

Right!

Lifting her into his arms, Sean zoomed away through the back-door just before firefighters entered the kitchen. He was going to have to somehow make sure any blood samples taken from the blood on the floor, wouldn't lead back to Alexis, but that was a problem for another day. He stopped at a local park one minute later and placed her on the ground under a copse of trees. The first step is to drain her of blood, though she had already lost so much, that part was definitely out.

I can't lose her. I won't.

Second step, feed her vampire blood. He bit deeply into his wrist and placed it over Alexis' mouth.

Nothing happened.

Please work. This has to work.

Her heart was fighting, but it wasn't going to hold out much longer. She needed to be able to heal. He yanked the knife out of her chest, bit into his other wrist, and placed that over the wound. "Alexis. You better not die on me. You hear me? I promised you eternity and I plan to give that to you. I'm sorry our plans are ruined again. I wanted you to have such a memorable transition. Dammit! Why didn't I just change you that first night and been done with it? If I lose you because of my stupid plans, I will never forgive myself. Pretend my blood is your morning coffee and drink it alread—"

Her lips fastened around his wrist sucking as the earth began snaking up her body like veins. Relief, profound relief, flooded his whole body with power and he sensed her newly forming power emanate from her. *Thank fuck!* It was working and her eyes finally opened. Brown hungry eyes devouring him even as she devoured his blood. The dirt was stitching up her wounds and infusing her whole body with the special Earth magic that was part and parcel of being a vampire.

Once the dirt receded and her heart beat for the last time, he knew he'd done it.

"Alexis?"

"Coffee? Really? I mean your blood was good, but coffee? I don't think so. But, um, thanks for saving my life, bestie." Her impish grin was in full effect. If she could tease him like this, she was definitely okay.

He took a very necessary but unnecessary deep breath and grabbed her chin, tilting her beloved face to his. "Do you know how many years you took off my immortal life, Troublemaker?"

"Your math isn't mathing, but I know how upset I would have been and appreciate your loving me." She leaned in and, blood, dirt, and all, kissed him deeply.

The next thing he knew, she was in his lap and rocking her core against his sudden erection. "We can't do that here."

"I had no idea how horny being a vampire can be. With all my senses heightened, I only meant to kiss you, but I fucking need you right now. I mean that. Now."

She continued to grind. He was going to lose this fight and they would end up exposing themselves in a public space. It was one thing when they were quiet and on the ground, but sitting up and moaning, yeah, that was not going to work. Sean gathered her to him again and went hunting, not for an arsonist this time, but for reasons no less combustible.

[10]

CONFLAGRATION

Alexis felt utterly out of control. "I am so mad at you," she whispered.

"What?" Sean hissed back while zooming through shadows, taking them deeper into the forest.

"Now that I know how hard it is to control myself with your scent and taste, how the hell did you stay away from me for two long years?" She might sound just a tiny bit petulant, but come on, he should *not* have been able to keep his hands off of her. "Oomph."

They came to an abrupt halt as Sean slammed her back against a tree, not so it hurt—well, not much could probably hurt her now —but firmly trapped between it and his body. It felt good. Real good.

"Do you know how many times I've had to masturbate these last two years?" He pointed at himself with his eyebrows indignantly high and looking thoroughly put out.

It was hard, but she somehow restrained herself from laughing. He probably wouldn't like it.

He continued while waving his hand for emphasis. "I have vampire speed and healing. My hand was basically glued to my dick every time we hung out and speaking of my dick, it practically caught third-degree burns from the abuse. And you're mad at me? Wait. Are… Are you laughing?" He narrowed his eyes at her and that was the last straw.

She laughed harder. There was nothing for it. When she finally sobered, she rubbed the back of his neck to help soothe his tension, "Do you think I could possibly watch?"

"What?" His brows furrowed. But, his neck muscles began to relax at her touch.

"I want to watch you fuck your hand to the thought of me. To desiring me. Perhaps even while watching me. I want to see you come. I want to feel your power surge flow through me knowing it exists for me." His semi-hard cock came roaring back to fully erect life against her crotch. And, speaking of a crotch, Sean moved swiftly and her leggings no longer had anything in that region. Her underwear seemed to be missing a central piece as well.

One good swipe deserved another. She reached down between their bodies and using her new strength, wrenched open his pants, button flying and zipper ruined. His straining erection was popping out over his boxer briefs, so she reached in and gave it a few good strokes on the side near his body while also rubbing her pussy along his length on the other side. His head dropped down on her shoulder as he said, "You are trying to kill me."

"Aren't we both already undead? What I'm trying to do is drive you wild with lust." Alexis slipped just the tip of his cock in and hovered. "I want you fully primal now that you no longer have to be gentle with me. Fuck me, Sean."

Sean got the hint and slammed home in one hard thrust of his hips. They both gasped as their energies collided and began swirling together.

"Fuck, Alexis. You're mine. You're mine for infinity." He emphasized every word with the movement of his hips. "Say it. Tell me your mine." He twined his hand in her curls and yanked, positioning her head so she was forced to look him in the eye. "Tell me. I want to hear it. I almost lost you and I need to hear it."

"Yours. All yours. An eternity of yours." The heat of the moment engulfed her in its embrace.

"You're damn right you are."

His mouth claimed hers in a fierce kiss and she felt plundered above and below in the best way. She'd loved this man for as long as she could remember. Through some pretty awkward stages and challenging experiences, it had always been him. Going feral with him was one more right thing to experience with her other half.

"You're mine too, you know."

"Oh, I know it. Your energy compliments mine as though they are one. Can you feel it?"

"Yes!" And, she did. It was like nothing she'd ever experienced before. It permeated every part of her, but that wasn't all. The force rose in strength and swirled together, like lovers dancing around a bonfire.

"Come for me. Let go." He bit her, flooding her with even more pleasure.

She was about to do as he commanded. The pleasure was so intense, so complete, so overpowering and she was the tourniquet holding back the flow and letting it build up. For one torturous moment, she held herself suspended on the precipice of pleasure. The next, she released her hold and it was like the world dropped away and all that was left was them. Her shuddering in pleasure while her power shot out, rattling the trees and leaves.

Sean was pumping furiously into her. Meanwhile, Alexis' teeth elongated which was a weird sensation she would think more on later. She bit him back. His hiss told her that her novice bite had hurt. His subsequent moan told her she'd figured out how to release the chemical that made it feel good. It didn't take long before he grunted and came. Gradually coming to a stop and holding her close.

"Alexis."

She licked at her bite mark, healing it, and said, "Yes?"

"Marry me."

"What?" *He did not say what I think he—*

"Marry me?"

"Are you seriously asking me to marry you dick deep against a tree?"

"Yeeessss? In my defense, making elaborate plans doesn't work for us. I thought I would be spontaneous."

"You have a point there." She ran her fingers into his hair and pulled his head back so she could look him in the eyes when she responded. "Yes. Yes, I'll marry you but I have one condition."

His lopsided grin was so adorable as he questioned, "And what's that?"

"We elope. Like you said, plans are not our thing."

She winked and then yelped as he pulled her from the tree and spun her around in celebration. His legs tangled in the pants around his ankles and they dropped to the ground with her astride him and she realized that he was hard. Again? Or, still?

She could have sworn they'd exhausted each other already, but no, every fiber of her body wanted to ride him right now.

Sean must have felt the same way because he gripped her hips and hissed between clenched teeth, "Do it."

A couple of orgasms, bites, and power surges later, she was s. p. e. n. t. Spent. Sean vampire zoomed them back to his apartment. From there he proceeded to take such good care of her. He washed her head to toe, dried and moisturized or maintained every inch, and then placed her in his bed in a cocoon of soft silk sheets. Some time passed and he climbed into bed with her smelling all clean himself. She cuddled right into the crook of his arm.

"Where'd you go? That took you a minute." She played, rubbing her finger tip over every ridge, learning every line from his pecs to his six-pack.

"I set up the coffee machine so it would have coffee ready in the morning, exactly how you like it. You may be a vampire now, but I'm sure there are things about you that will never change."

He said that so casually, but honestly, nothing could have prepared her for how loved she felt. "I love you, Sean."

"I love you, Alexis, so damn much."

"An eternity of love. I'm holding you to it."

He squeezed her to him. "Yes. And, an eternity for me to

worship this body." He flipped her onto her back and proceeded to do so with his mouth. An eternity might not be enough.

And the dress? Well, sadly, the perfect dress didn't last an eternity.

Only the perfect, loving friendship could do that.

EPILOGUE: HOT

From: iByte@ibytemore.com
To: Sean.Buttler@gobblemail.com
Re: Glad to see you're okay

Hiya Sean,

I hope everything went smoothly with you and Alexis. Your follow-up request about turning someone seems to indicate it did. I always knew you were meant for each other. I'm not sure why you were both so stubborn it took you this long to get together. I'm happy to discuss how to turn someone when you are ready. Maybe we can get on a Faceall soon to talk it out.

I'm afraid we are dealing with some unrest in our part of the world and it's not coming from the aliens this time. LOL I'm practically a Staraban marketing manager at this point. Who would have thunk? Amiright?

Anyway, as I said, things are heating up in the region and I'm not sure what happens next. My new friend Jill is on a special mission. We're still unraveling the plot with the Vrolan. Our scientists are working on some science-y things to see what they can learn. Things are changing quickly.

Thank you for your offer to help. I'll definitely keep you updated on any developments. I hope it won't come to it, but if there is a need, you can bet I'll put out the bat call to all of the supernatural world, especially my friends. Thanks in advance, if it is necessary. Let's hope it doesn't come to that. The Vrolan are a pain to kill and some have some pretty nasty surprise attacks. Let's just say I learned that the hard way.

I also have something brewing with Hal but, shhh, that's a secret for now. Let's just say I can't wait for you to talk to him afterward.

Say hello to Alexis for me and we'll get her changed in the romantic, peaceful, memorable way you are planning.

Your friend,
Jack

EXCERPT OF CLAIMING JILL
CHAPTER 1: THE JILL ELEMENT

Fuck-It-All Diary Entry
October 21, 2025
Dear Diary,

I can't believe I've been talked into doing this, but whatever. My new friend Rory suggested I create you, so here you are. Apparently, she thinks I need to therapize or some shit. She *thinks* I should get my thoughts out somewhere because I've supposedly "been through a lot" lately.

Bitch, please. My childhood, now that was a lot.

And, okay, now that it's Nial and me alone for the next twelve days on a small spaceship returning back to Earth, it's possible and even probable that I will need someone to talk to who won't turn every conversation into a screaming match.

Fair.

The main reason I feel compelled to get you started though, is to keep a record of all the wild shit I've learned of lately. I mean, if what I've experienced just in the first few weeks of knowing this new group of friends and learning about life outside of a militia, who knows what might come next?

It all started the day I decided to defect from MAD. For reference, that's the militia group I was raised in. You see… my dear old dad is the leader and my mom died when I was quite young.

It's also the same group currently trying to kill all the aliens back on Earth. It's in the freaking name, Make Aliens Dead. Real original, right? Dad's skills are *not* in creative names, but more in creative ways to be devious, underhanded, or cruel. Yep, he has all the best qualities in a dad.

Did I mention that I'd heard that since my defection, he's issued a command that I be killed on sight? Yeah… Dad of the mother-fucking year.

And, now? Now, he's the reason I have to prematurely end my space adventure. There I was, finally having a good time. Rory and I shooting the shit as we stowed away undetected for days on Bren's ship. Getting caught could have been the end of it, but nope, things somehow had gotten even better.

We were training on weapons and learning the fighting techniques of the Staraban. Did I mention that's the name of the aliens? Anyway, it was heaven compared to my upbringing. Training in a facility where people respect each other instead of beating each other to a pulp? Radical. Learning a skill without someone telling you you're trash every time you don't quite get it yet? That's alternate reality-type stuff. If I was someone who could get giddy, I would have.

Okay, sure, one could say I had a near-death experience, so it wasn't all good. But I didn't die and that wasn't the first near-death experience I've had, so all-in-all a positive outcome in my book. I recovered and was looking forward to rejoining Rory and the rest of the crew doing space travel, warrior shit.

But noooo… Dear old dad had to go and ruin *this* for me too. He's threatening death and destruction back on Earth. Yeah. So, here we are. Heading back to Earth instead of exploring space. To say I'm angry about it, well, truth be told, I was already angry at him before all of this. Can't get more angry than wanting to end someone, I figure.

To top all this, I'm heading back with Nial. The alien who

angers, challenges, disturbs, and fascinates me in equal measures. He volunteered to be my pilot and I had no say in the matter. Not that I know what I would have said if given the option. Did I mention how complicated my feelings are where he's concerned?

Well, I met *him* the day I defected, too, assuming you call getting tackled by an alien "a meeting."

I just realized I haven't explained all that has been going down lately. Oops. My bad. I guess you could say the day I defected changed everything.

The rundown goes like this: escaped from the militia by capturing an alien and a fucking vampire. Yes… you heard me, a fucking vampire! I realized they were my ticket out, which is a much longer story. There was a lot of arguing by the prisoners and I shot some people, but not them. I digress. Anyway… I ended up befriending that fucking vampire, Jack, as well as her best friend Rory, whom I've mentioned multiple times. That bitch Rory, and I mean that in the best way, turned out to be a shifter because, of course she did. I'm still waiting for my introduction to a zombie and a fairy.

Too much happened to go into, but some important information needed to be taken from Earth to the All Alien Alliance or AAA. For frustrating reasons, Rory and I had to stow away on their mother-fucking ship that looked like a clam with horns and a tail. Not exactly a best design winner in my book. When the mutant-clam-ship was attacked, I got up close and personal with a very sharp knife. One near-miss meeting with the grim reaper later, and I learned my dear psychopathic dad was still a total asshole.

Just another day that ends in "y" with my dad.

That said, I admit he's taking things to a whole new level by kidnapping and threatening to hurt innocent people, which is why Tarc and Jack requested *my* help to stop him. They're working with local authorities but no one knows him, his crew, or those mountains quite like me.

And, that is why, dear FIA, I'm heading back to Earth, on a small ship called D-ROMP, to deal with his sorry ass. Permanently. At least, that's *my* plan.

So, FIA—Can I call you FIA? Of course I can. You may be wondering how I'm coping with all of this. The answer is in your name.

Hey. I think I do feel a bit better. This might just be good for me after all. Look at me getting all therapized and in touch with my feels or some shit.

Fuck. It. All.
Spikey

ABOUT THE AUTHOR

Michelle Mars has an unhealthy obsession with coffee, caramel, and funny t-shirts. This single mom of two amazing, kind, and creative dragons/children has naturally purple hair and loves nothing more than talking books, kids, and living your best life. She enjoys reading romance, traveling, and writing stories that make her readers laugh, sweat, and swoon.

Author of the steamy, paranormal, sci-fi, romcom Love Wars Series; Moving Jack, Adoring Alexis, Chasing Rory, Embracing Irina, and Claiming Jill out now. Loving Will is later this year.

And, the contemporary romcom series, The Frisky Bean; Frisky Intentions, the short story prequel, Frisky Connections, and Frisky Collections Volume 1, Frisky and Queer out now. Frisky Business is coming soon.

Michelle's truth: Humor is a turn-on!

For updates go to www.michellemars.com and register to her newsletter.

ALSO BY MICHELLE MARS

Moving Jack, Love Wars Book 1

You can buy the above cover in print signed by me from my website www. michellemars.com.

Chasing Rory, Love Wars Book 2

You can buy the above cover in print signed by me from my website www.
michellemars.com.

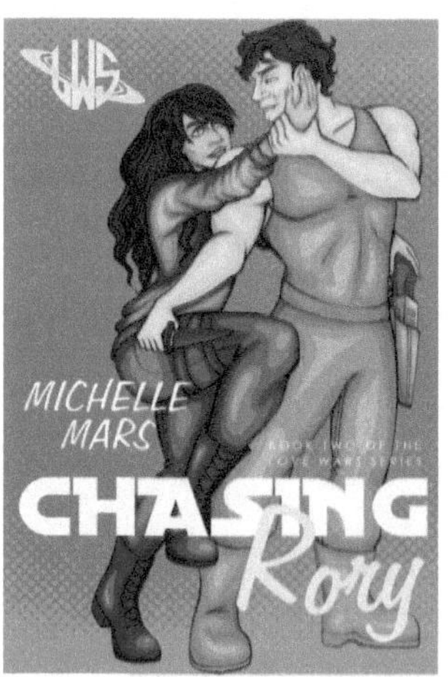

Embracing Irina, Love Wars Book 0.5 Prequel

You can buy the above cover in print signed by me from my website www.
michellemars.com.

Claiming Jill, Love Wars Book 3

You can buy the above cover in print signed by me from my website www. michellemars.com.

MICHELLE MARS
CLAIMING Jill
BOOK THREE OF THE
LOVE WARS SERIES

<u>Other Work:</u>

Frisky Connections

Frisky
Intentions
THE FRISKY
BEAN
THE FRISKY
BEAN
MICHELLE MARS

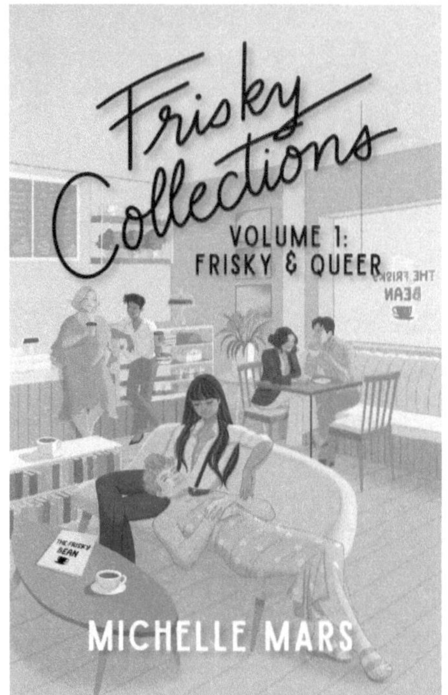

Frisky Collections
VOLUME 1:
FRISKY & QUEER
THE FRISKY BEAN
THE FRISKY BEAN
MICHELLE MARS

www.ingramcontent.com/pod-product-compliance
Lightning Source LLC
Chambersburg PA
CBHW030845200726

48285CB00007B/2558